Miss Mary Is Scary!

Dan Gutman

Pictures by
Jim Paillot

HARPER

An Imprint of HarperCollinsPublishers

To Emma

Miss Mary Is Scary!

Text copyright © 2010 by Dan Gutman

Illustrations copyright © 2010 by Jim Paillot

All rights reserved. Printed in the United States of America.

Library of Congress Cataloging-in-Publication Data is available.

ISBN 978-0-06-170398-0 (lib. bdg.)—ISBN 978-0-06-170397-3 (pbk.)

Typography by Joel Tippie

13 14   CG/BR   10 9 8

❖

First Edition

Contents

A Ghost in the Bathroom

My name is A.J. and I hate school.

It was a couple of weeks before Halloween, which is the coolest holiday of the year. We get to wear our costumes to school on Halloween and have a big candy party. At the end of the day we parade around the block with all the parents watching.

Marching in a parade is way better than watching a parade, because you don't have to stand in one place for a million hundred hours.

"Hang up your coats in the cloakroom," said my teacher, Mr. Granite, who is from another planet.

What a weird name for a room: "cloakroom." Who wears a *cloak*? I don't even know what a cloak is.

After we finished circle time and Word of the Day, Mr. Granite told us to take out our math books and turn to page twenty-three.

"Can I go to the bathroom?" I asked.

"Do you really need to, A.J.?" said Mr. Granite.

"Yes!"

I didn't *really* need to go to the bathroom. Sometimes I go to the bathroom even though I don't have to. Like when Mr. Granite is teaching math. I hate math. Math is the perfect time to go to the bathroom.

"Arlo doesn't need to go to the bathroom," said Andrea Young, this annoying girl with curly brown hair. She calls me by my real name because she knows I don't like it.

"I do too."

"Do not."

We went back and forth like that for a while. But the teachers *have* to let you go to the bathroom. It's a law. If they don't let you go to the bathroom, they have to go to jail.

"Go ahead, A.J.," Mr. Granite grumbled.

"The boys' bathroom is haunted, y'know," whispered my friend Ryan. "I heard there's a ghost in there."

"Yeah, watch out for that ghost," said my friend Michael. "He eats kids for lunch."

That's ridiculous. There's no such thing as a ghost. And even if there were ghosts, they wouldn't go to the bathroom. They don't *have* to.

Even if ghosts *did* have to go to the bathroom, they wouldn't *haunt* one. Ghosts haunt graveyards, basements, and old houses of people who died. Not bathrooms. Everybody knows that. I'm not afraid of ghosts.

Still, I was going to be careful, just to be on the safe side. I walked down the hall and pushed open the door to the bathroom.*

"Anybody in here?" I asked.

Nobody answered.

I sat down in one of the stalls. There was nothing to do, but it was better than learning math.

That's when something really weird happened. The toilet in the stall next to me flushed.

"Who's in there?" I asked, alarmed.

---

*What are you looking down here for? The story's up there, dumbhead!

Nobody answered.

I peeked under the stall to see who was in there.

Nobody.

"Are you a . . . ghost?" I asked.

The ghost didn't answer. Maybe it was invisible.

I picked up the extra roll of toilet paper in case I had to hit the invisible ghost over the head with it.

That's when something even *weirder* happened. The toilet on the *other* side of me flushed!

"Who *is* that?" I demanded.

Nobody answered.

I peeked under the stall.

Nobody was there.

This was *really* weird! Maybe there were *two* invisible ghosts! And they had me surrounded! I was scared. I wanted to run away to Antarctica and go live with the penguins.

But that's when the weirdest thing in the history of the world happened. The toilet I was sitting on suddenly flushed!

"AHHHHHHHHHHHHHHHH!"

I got up and ran out of the stall. Then I ran past the sinks, and *they* turned on! Then I ran past the hand dryer, and *it* turned on!

"Help!" I screamed as I ran out the door. "There are ghosts in there!"

I ran back to class and shouted, "There are ghosts in the bathroom! Help!"

"Calm down, A.J.," Mr. Granite told me. "What happened?"

"I was in the stall," I explained, "and the toilet on my left flushed all by itself! And then the toilet on my right flushed all by itself! And then the toilet I was sitting on flushed all by itself! And the sinks and hand dryer turned on too! But nobody was there! It must be ghosts! The bathroom is haunted! Run for your lives!"

Everybody started freaking out, yelling, screaming, and crying.

That's when our custodian, Miss Lazar, came in.

"There are no ghosts in the bathroom," Miss Lazar said. "I recently installed automatic sinks, hand dryers, and toilets to save water and electricity. I was just testing them out to see if they work."

Oh.

Well, maybe there aren't any ghosts in the bathroom after all. But I'm not going in there again for the rest of my life.

The New Student Teacher

Mr. Granite told us that it was *his* idea to install the new water-saving toilets.

"Every time you flush a toilet," he said, "you use up to 5 gallons of water. So five flushes in a day would be . . . five times five—25 gallons of water a day . . ."

Mr. Granite loves math.

". . . and that adds up to 175 gallons a week," Mr. Granite continued. "And 9,100 gallons a year. And do you know how many gallons of water you will flush down the toilet in your lifetime?"

He didn't have the chance to answer the question, because at that moment the weirdest thing in the history of the world happened. The door opened.

Well, that's not the weird part because doors open all the time. But you'll never believe who walked into the door.

Nobody, because if you walked into a door it would hurt. But you'll never believe who walked into the *doorway*.

It was our principal, Mr. Klutz!

He has no hair at all. I think Mr. Klutz used to have hair, but it fell out a long time ago. That's what happens when men get old.

He held up his hand and made a peace sign, which means "shut up."

"I have big news!" he told us.

"Mr. Klutz has a big nose," I whispered to Ryan, who sits next to me.

"What is it?" asked Andrea's crybaby friend, Emily.

"You're going to get a student teacher!" Mr. Klutz announced. "Isn't that exciting?"

"Yes!" said all the girls.

"No!" said all the boys.

Wait a minute. *Student teacher?* That

doesn't make any sense.

"How can a student be a teacher?" I asked. "Or a teacher be a student? A person can either be a student or a teacher, but not both."

"A student teacher is somebody who's learning how to *be* a teacher, dumbhead," said Andrea.

"Oh, snap!" said Ryan.

"So is your face," I told Andrea.

Any time somebody says something mean to you and you can't think of what to say, just say, "So is your face." That's the first rule of being a kid.

"What is our student teacher's name?" Andrea asked. "When will we meet her?"

"Right now!" Mr. Klutz said. "Come on in here, Mary. Don't be shy. Kids, this is your new student teacher, Miss Mary."

A lady came in. She looked weird. She had black hair, black clothes, black eye makeup, and a tattoo of a black bat on her arm. There was a purple streak in her hair. She had holes in her pants and ear-buds in her ears.

She was chewing gum and bobbing her head up and down to the music.

Mr. Granite didn't look very happy when he saw Miss Mary.

"Yo," she said as she took out one of her earbuds. "What up?"

"Yo," we all replied.

"Miss Mary is going to be a great teacher," Mr. Klutz told us. "Do you know how I know she'll be so good?"

"How?" we all asked.

"Because," Mr. Klutz said as he put his arm around her, "Mary is my daughter."

WHAT?!

Miss Mary Is Weird

Mr. Klutz has a *daughter*? I knew he was married to a lady named Mrs. Klutz. But I didn't know they had kids.

Mr. Klutz told us that a long time ago, before he was married to Mrs. Klutz, he was married to some other lady in England and they had a baby. So Miss Mary grew up in England and came to America for a year to do her student teaching.

"Isn't she lovely?" he said.

"Yes!" we all lied. Nobody wanted to tell Mr. Klutz that his daughter looked weird.

"Well, I have to go to a meeting," Mr. Klutz said. "Mary, I'm so glad you decided to become a teacher and help educate the youth of America so they can pursue their hopes and dreams."

"Yeah, whatever," said Miss Mary.

"I'll stop back in a little while to see how you're making out," Mr. Klutz said before he left.

Ugh, disgusting! Mr. Klutz said "making out"!

Mr. Granite had a frowny face. He looked like he didn't want to have a student teacher.

"So, Miss Mary," he said, "what made you decide to become a teacher?"

"Well, it's like, the kids, y'know," she said. "They're so, I don't know. Kidlike. You know? Yeah, and when you're a teacher, you get the summer off, right? That's cool."

People from England talk funny. Miss Mary sounded like she should be in a Harry Potter movie.

"Yes, I do get the summer off," Mr. Granite said. "But most people become teachers for other reasons, like . . ."

He didn't get the chance to finish his sentence because suddenly loud music started playing. Everybody looked around to see where it was coming from.

"Hang on," Miss Mary said. "It's my bloody cell phone."

"Your cell phone is covered with blood?" I asked.

"I gotta take this," Mary said. "It's my boyfriend, Zack."

Mr. Granite looked mad. Cell phones aren't allowed in school. But I guess he couldn't do anything about it, because Miss Mary is Mr. Klutz's daughter.

"Yo! What up, dude?" Miss Mary said into the phone. "I'm at Daddy's school. . . ."

I miss you, too, Zack. . . . Okay, gotta go. . . . Later."

"Are you quite finished?" asked Mr. Granite. "I'd like to do our math lesson."

"Yeah," Miss Mary said. "Zack is back home in England. He says he's coming over here even though his parents don't like me."

"Gee, I wonder why," Mr. Granite said. "Okay, open your math books to page twenty-three, shall we?"

We all opened our math books.

"Zack is in an awesome band called Fish Food," Miss Mary said. "They totally rock."

"Music is my favorite thing!" said Andrea. "I love the Jonas Brothers."

"Me too!" said Emily, who loves everything that Andrea loves.

"Zack is into heavy metal," said Miss Mary.

"He wears a suit of armor?" I asked.

"Heavy metal is a kind of music, dumbhead," said Andrea, rolling her eyes.

"I knew that," I lied.

"Zack is a genius," Miss Mary said. "He'll be famous someday. We want to get married. But Daddy won't let us. He says Zack can't earn a living by playing music."

Mr. Granite's face was all red. He doesn't like it when we get off task. But it didn't matter, because that's when something really weird happened.

A guy climbed in the window!

Everybody was freaking out. The guy was dressed all in black, just like Mary.

"Zack!" yelled Miss Mary.

"Mary!" yelled Zack.

"I thought you called from England!" Miss Mary said.

"No, I was right around the corner," said Zack.

"I love you!"

"I love you, too!"

Ugh. They said the
L word! Miss Mary and
Zack started smooching.
I thought I was gonna throw up.

"Isn't it romantic?" said Andrea. "Zack
and Miss Mary are in love, but their parents won't let them be together. It's just

like *Romeo and Juliet*!"

"This is strictly against school rules," Mr. Granite said.

"Please don't tell Daddy that Zack is here," Miss Mary begged Mr. Granite. "Please?"

Suddenly, there was the sound of footsteps outside the door.

"It's Mr. Klutz!" Ryan shouted.

"Hide, Zack!" said Miss Mary.

"Where?" asked Zack.

"In the cloakroom!" Mr. Granite told him.

Zack ran into the cloakroom and shut the door. Mr. Klutz came into the room.

"So," he said, "how are you making out, Mary?"

"Ugh, disgusting!" I said.

"I'm making out just fine, Daddy!" Miss Mary said.

"Good," said Mr. Klutz. "I'll check up on you again later."

Whew! That was a close one!

4

Bog Snorkeling and Cheese Rolling

After Mr. Klutz left, Zack came out of the cloakroom.

"Thanks, dude," he told Mr. Granite. "If old man Klutz finds out I'm here with Mary, he'll have me bloody head."

"I don't see any blood on your head," I told Zack.

"People in England say the word 'bloody' all the time, Arlo," Andrea told me. "Zack just means that Mr. Klutz will be angry if he finds him here with Miss Mary."

That's sure a weird way to say it.

"I thought people in England were always saying 'Chip, chip, cheerio, old chap,'" said Michael. "I saw that in a movie."

"Nobody *ever* says 'Chip, chip, cheerio,'" said Miss Mary.

"I guess we have a lot to learn about England," said Mr. Granite.

"Does everybody in England dress like you two?" asked Ryan. "Or are those your Halloween costumes?"

"This is how I always dress," said Zack. "My favorite color is black."

"Mine too," said Miss Mary. "I love black spiders and insects. They're my friends. Back home I have a black bat named Roger."

Miss Mary is scary.

"Black isn't even a color," said Neil, who we call the nude kid even though he wears clothes.

"How did your pants get ripped like that?" asked Emily. "Did you get caught climbing a fence?"

"Oh no. I used a pair of scissors," said Miss Mary. "Don't my pants look fierce?"

"I could darn them for you," Andrea

told her. "I took a sewing class after school last year."*

"No thanks," said Zack and Miss Mary.

"Maybe you'd like to tell the children a little bit about what life is like in England," suggested Mr. Granite.

We all crowded around Miss Mary and Zack.

"Well, my friends and I really love to go bog snorkeling," Zack said.

"Bog snorkeling?" asked Neil. "What's *that*?"

"It's when you snorkel through a bog," Zack told us.

---

*Andrea takes classes in *everything* after school. If they gave a class on tying your shoes, she would take that class so she could get better at it.

"My friends and I love cheese rolling," said Miss Mary.

"Let me guess," I said. "You roll cheese?"

"Yes!" said Miss Mary. "It happens on the Spring Bank Holiday. The cheese roller will roll a round cheese down a hill, and we all chase it. The winner is the first person to grab the cheese."

"It sounds very dangerous," said Andrea.

"Oh, it is," said Miss Mary. "One time I got a bloody nose."

"But your nose wasn't *really* bloody, right?" I asked. "You just say the word 'bloody' all the time."

"No, my nose really was bloody," Miss Mary said.

"Of *course* it was bloody, Arlo!" Andrea told me.

I guess if it wasn't bloody, Miss Mary would have just gotten a nose. And that wouldn't make any sense. You can't get a nose. Everybody already has a nose.

I was confused.

"Hey, I gotta split, man," said Zack. "I'm working on a new song with my band, Fish Food."

"Oooh, what's the song called?" asked Emily.

"It's called 'I Love Dirt,'" Zack replied.

What?! Who writes songs about dirt? Zack climbed out the window and left. People from England are weird.

Learning More About England

The next morning Halloween decorations were up in the hallways. I came into class and hung my coat in the cloakroom. Miss Mary was sitting in the back of the class.

We usually have Word of the Day first thing in the morning, but Mr. Granite said we would skip it so we could do the math lesson we missed the day before.

"Open your math books to page twenty-three," Mr. Granite told us. But suddenly he stopped, looked at Miss Mary, and asked, "What are you doing?"

We all looked at Miss Mary. She was holding her cell phone.

"I'm texting Zack," she said. "He just told me 'I Love Dirt' is going to be the best song he ever wrote. And he's dedicating it to *me*! I can't wait to hear it."

"That's so romantic!" said Andrea.

"Turn off your cell phone in school, please," said Mr. Granite.

He looked all frustrated. That's when

an announcement came over the loud-speaker.

"Mr. Granite, please come to the office."

"Another interruption!" he said. "We may *never* get to math. Miss Mary, will you take over the class while I'm gone?"

He went rushing out of the room. We all looked at Miss Mary.

"So, what do you want to learn?" she asked.

"We don't want to learn anything," I told her. "We want to go to recess."

"It's not time for recess, Arlo!" Andrea said, rolling her eyes.

"I can teach you how to play cricket," said Miss Mary.

"You play with crickets?" I said. "That's disgusting!"

"Cricket is a *game*, Arlo," Andrea said, rolling her eyes again. "They play it in England."

"Your face is a game," I told her.

"Can you show us where England is on the map?" asked Emily.

"Uh, sure," Miss Mary said, going to the map on the wall. "Let's see; where is that bloody country?"

"The country is bloody?" I asked.

Miss Mary looked all over, but she couldn't find England. And it's her own country! She's almost as dumb as the teacher we had last year, Miss Daisy.

"I'll show you," said Andrea as she
hopped out of her seat and pointed at the
map. "It's right *here*. England looks a little
like a microscope. See?"

"Very good, Andrea!" said Miss Mary.

Little Miss Smarty Pants smiled her know-it-all smile. Why can't a microscope fall on her head?

"What do people eat in England?" asked Ryan, who will eat anything, even stuff that isn't food.

"I love blood pudding," said Miss Mary.

"You make pudding out of *blood*?" I asked.

"Ewwwwww!" everybody went.

"Blood pudding is a kind of sausage," said Miss Mary.

"You should just call it sausage," said Michael.

"I also love fish and chips," Miss Mary said, "and bangers and mash."

"Bangers?" Neil asked. "What's a banger?"

"That's a kind of sausage too," Miss Mary told us.

"Why don't you just call sausage 'sausage'?" I suggested.

"People sure eat a lot of sausage in England," Andrea said.

"Well, what do you Americans like to eat?" asked Miss Mary.

"I like hot dogs," said Michael.

"You heat up dogs and eat them?" asked Miss Mary. "How horrid! In England dogs are our pets. We would never eat them."

"No!" I told her. "We don't eat dogs here either! A hot dog is sort of like . . . a sausage."

"Then why don't you call it a sausage?" asked Miss Mary.

"Beats me," I said.

"I guess everybody likes sausage," said Ryan, "but nobody wants to call it sausage."

"Say, can I tell you kids a secret?" asked Miss Mary.

"Yeah!" we all shouted.

"We love secrets," Andrea said.

"Promise you won't tell?" asked Miss Mary.

"We promise."

"I don't really want to be a teacher," Miss Mary whispered. "I want to go on tour with Zack and his band. But don't tell Daddy. He'll be so disappointed."

"We won't tell," we all promised.

I couldn't blame Miss Mary for not wanting to be a teacher. Who would want to go to school for the rest of your life? When I grow up, I'm not going anywhere *near* a school.

Suddenly, the most amazing thing in the history of the world happened. Zack climbed in the window.

"Zack!"

"Mary!"

They started smooching. Ugh, disgusting!

"Can I hear your song 'I Love Dirt'?" Miss Mary asked.

"Not yet," Zack replied. "It's not finished."

"But I want to hear it *now*!"

"Soon, sweetie. Soon."

"Boo hoo!"

Miss Mary started crying. Her black eye makeup was running down her face.

Suddenly, there were footsteps in the hall.

"It might be Mr. Klutz!" yelled Neil the nude kid.

"Hide, Zack!" Ryan shouted.

"Where?"

"In the bloody cloakroom!" said Michael.

"There's blood in the cloakroom?" I asked.

Zack ran into the cloakroom.

As it turned out, the footsteps weren't Mr. Klutz's at all. It was Mr. Granite, back from the office.

"You can come out, Zack," Miss Mary said.

Zack came out of the cloakroom.

"What are *you* doing here again?" Mr. Granite asked.

"I was worried about Mary," Zack told him. "She wasn't answering her cell phone."

"He made me turn it off," Mary explained.

"I'm glad you're okay. Look, I gotta get back to work," Zack said. "The song is almost done."

"Maybe now I can finally teach some math around here," said Mr. Granite.

"Bye, Zack!" said Miss Mary.

"Later," Zack said as he climbed out the window.

"So, what did you learn while I was

gone?" Mr. Granite asked us.

"We learned that in England they play with crickets," I told him, "and they make pudding out of blood."

Vampires Are Cute

Mr. Granite didn't have the chance to teach his math lesson, because it was time for lunch. We walked single file to the vomitorium. Neil the nude kid was the line leader.

I sat with the guys, and we were talking about Halloween. We were all going

46

as superheroes. I would be Batman. Ryan would be Superman. Michael would be Spider-Man. Neil would be the Invisible Man.

"Who do you think would win in a fight?" Michael asked. "Superman or Batman?"

"Superman would win," said Ryan. "He could burn Batman up with his heat vision in a second."

"No way," I told him. "Batman would pull out a little mirror, and the heat vision would bounce back and burn Superman alive."

"Superman is invulnerable to heat," Ryan told me.

"Not if it comes from his own eyes," I insisted. "It would kill him."

"Would not."

"Would too."

We went back and forth like that for a while. Andrea and her girly friends were at the next table, listening to our important discussion.

"Boys are dumbheads," said Andrea.

"Oh, yeah?" I said. "What are *you* dressing up as for Halloween? Beach Blanket Barbie?"

"No," Andrea replied. "I'm going as Steven Spielberg."

What?!

"Who's Steven Spielberg?" asked Neil the nude kid.

"He's a famous movie director," Andrea told us. "I take a moviemaking class after school. My parents even let me use their video camera so I can make my own movies. We're going to put them on YouTube."

"You should make a movie about Miss

Mary," said Michael. "It could be a horror movie."

"Yeah," Neil said. "She looks like a vampire."

"Maybe she really *is* a vampire," I whispered to everybody. "Did you ever think of that? She dresses all in black. She wears black makeup. She's got a pet bat. She even eats blood pudding!"

"Wow!" said Ryan. "I think you might be right, A.J.!"

"Stop trying to scare Emily," Andrea told me.

"I'm scared," said Emily, looking all worried.

"Miss Mary probably lives in a cave and sleeps hanging upside down from the ceiling," I said. "Then she goes out at night and bites people on the neck and drinks their blood."

"We've got to *do* something!" Emily yelled, and then she went running out of the room.

Sheesh, get a grip! That girl is such a crybaby.

"I *like* vampires," Andrea said. "I saw this movie about a vampire. He was really handsome, and all the girls fell in love with him. He looked a little like Zack."

"Why would girls fall in love with a guy who bites them on the neck and drinks their blood?" I asked.

"Because he's cute!" Andrea said. "Like Zack."

"You think Zack is cute?" I snorted.

"Arlo, I think you're jealous!" said Andrea, all smiley.

My face started to feel warm.

"I am *not* jealous!" I told her. "If you ask me, Zack looks more like a zombie than a vampire anyway."

"Ooooooh!" Ryan said. "A.J. is jealous because Andrea thinks Zack is cute. He must be in *love* with her!"

"When are you gonna get married?" asked Michael.

If those guys weren't my best friends, I would hate them.

I Love Dirt

The next day, first thing in the morning, we had show-and-tell. I brought in some of my Matchbox cars. Ryan brought in a model plane he built from a kit. Andrea brought in her parents' video camera that she uses to shoot movies.

"Okay," Mr. Granite said after show-

and-tell was over. Now we can *finally* get to our math lesson. Turn to page twenty-three."

But we didn't get to our math lesson. Because at that moment, guess who climbed in the window?

"Zack!" shouted Mary.

"Mary!" shouted Zack.

"Not *again*!" shouted Mr. Granite. "Don't you ever use the door?"

"I love you!"

"I love you, too!"

Zack and Miss Mary started smooching, like always. Ugh, disgusting!

"They are *so* romantic!" said Andrea.

"Hey, I finished writing my song," Zack told Miss Mary. "Do you want to hear it?"

"Perhaps you can sing the song *after* school is over," suggested Mr. Granite. "We really need to work on math."

"I want to hear Zack's song *now*!" whined Miss Mary.

"So do we!" all the kids shouted.

"If you don't let Zack sing his song,"

Miss Mary told Mr. Granite, "I'm going to tell Daddy you're a bad teacher."

"Sing the song," Mr. Granite said, closing his eyes and rubbing his forehead.

"Yay!" everybody cheered.

"Can I film you with my video camera?" Andrea asked Zack.

"Sure!" he replied. Then he started rapping: ♫

"I love dirt! I love dirt!
♫   *I love dirt! I love dirt!"*

Zack motioned for us to chant with him. . . .

"I love dirt! I love dirt!
I love dirt! I love dirt!"

Then he started rapping:

"Now, some love Ernie,
and some love Bert,
And some love Big Bird;
but I love dirt!"

We all chanted:

"I love dirt! I love dirt!
I love dirt! I love dirt!"

Then Zack started rapping again:

"Now, some love dinner,
*   and some love dessert,*
And some love breakfast;
*   but I love dirt!"*

We all chanted:

"I love dirt! I love dirt!
*   I love dirt! I love dirt!"*

Then Zack started rapping again:

"Now, listen to me, '
*   cause I'm an expert.*

Don't freak out if you
        get it on your shirt.
I rub it on my face,
        I love gettin' dirty,

And I'll keep doin' it
        until I turn thirty."

We all chanted:

"I love dirt! I love dirt!
        I love dirt! I love dirt!"

Then Zack started rapping again:

"So when I'm dead
        and did my last concert,

Throw me in a hole
and cover it with dirt."

We all chanted:

"I love dirt! I love dirt!
I love dirt! I love dirt!"

Then Zack started rapping again:

"It doesn't hurt—I love dirt!
I'm here to assert—I love dirt!
I gotta blurt—I love dirt!
Don't mean to be curt—I love dirt!
I'm issuing an all points alert—
I love dirt!"

Zack took a bow. We all cheered and clapped.

"That song is *awesome*!" Miss Mary told Zack.

"I wrote it just for *you*," he replied.

"I think I'm going to cry!" said Miss Mary.

"That is *so* romantic!" Andrea said. "Would it be okay if I put this video up on YouTube?"

"Sure," said Zack. "That would be cool."

"Okay, can we get back to math now?" Mr. Granite said.

He told us to open our math books to page twenty-three. But at that moment there were footsteps in the hall.

"It's Mr. Klutz!" Neil the nude kid yelled.

"Hide, Zack!" Miss Mary shouted.

Zack ran into the cloakroom just before Mr. Klutz walked in the room.

"Is everything okay in here?" he asked. "I thought I heard somebody yelling."

"Uh, we were singing . . . 'Mary Had a Little Lamb,'" said Mr. Granite.

"That's odd," said Mr. Klutz. "I thought I heard something about dirt."

"A song about dirt?" asked Mr. Granite. "That's ridiculous! Why would anybody sing about dirt?"

Mr. Klutz was looking at Mr. Granite.

Mr. Granite looked at Miss Mary. Miss Mary looked at Andrea. Andrea looked at me.

I didn't know what to say. I didn't know what to do. I had to think fast.

"Maybe you're losing your hearing, Mr. Klutz," I said. "Hearing is a lot like hair. When men get old, they lose it."

Then I mouthed a few nonsense words without making any noise.

"What did you say, A.J.?" asked Mr. Klutz.

I mouthed some more nonsense words without making any noise.

"Hmmm," Mr. Klutz said. "Maybe I *am* losing my hearing. I didn't hear a word you said. I'd better go get my ears checked."

And then he left.

Everybody said I was a genius for convincing Mr. Klutz that he had hearing problems.* Ryan said I should get the No Bell Prize. That's a prize they give out to people who don't have bells.

---

*No wonder I'm in the gifted and talented program!

Zack's Big Nose

The next day was Friday. Mr. Granite didn't start the morning with Word of the Day like he usually does. We didn't do show-and-tell. We didn't even pledge the allegiance. Mr. Granite said he wanted to make sure we had time to work on math.

"Open your math books," he told us,

"and turn to page twenty-three."

I took my math book out of my desk. Bummer in the summer! We were actually going to have to do math, the most boring subject in the history of the world.

But that's when Zack climbed in the window.

Yay! No math!

"Zack!" shouted Miss Mary.

"Mary!" shouted Zack.

"Not *again*!" shouted Mr. Granite as he slammed his math book shut. "Zack, what are you doing here *now*? Why don't you save us all some time and go hide in the cloakroom?"

"I love you, Zack!" said Miss Mary.

"I love you, too!" said Zack.

They started smooching, of course. Ugh, disgusting!

"Those two are *so* romantic!" said Andrea.

"I'm sorry to interrupt your class, Mr. Granite," Zack said. "But I had to come in. I have big news!"

"Zack has a big nose," I whispered to Ryan.

"What is it?" we all asked. Mr. Granite sat at his desk. He looked tired.

"Y'know the video that Andrea shot of me singing 'I Love Dirt'?" Zack said.

"Yes," said Andrea. "My mom helped me upload it to YouTube after school yesterday."

"Well, it went viral!" Zack exclaimed.

"It went viral! It went viral! It went viral!" everybody started yelling.

Huh? What the heck does *that* mean? Going viral doesn't sound good. I had a virus once, and it made me throw up.

"Did you throw up?" I asked Zack.

"Going viral means that thousands of people saw the video!" Andrea said excitedly.

"Actually," Zack said, "*millions* of people saw it. Not only that, but last night I got a call from the producer of *Saturday Night Live*! He loved 'I Love Dirt'! He wants to fly me and Fish Food to New York so we can perform it on the show tomorrow night!"

"You're kidding me!" Miss Mary said, jumping up and down.

"I'm not kidding you!" said Zack, jumping up and down with her.

"You're joking!"

"I'm not joking!"

They went back and forth like that for a while. But finally, Zack convinced Miss Mary that it was true. Fish Food would be flying to New York to perform "I Love Dirt" on *Saturday Night Live*.

"That's wonderful, Zack!" Miss Mary yelled.

Everybody in the class was freaking out, jumping up and down and going crazy.

Well, everybody except Mr. Granite. He didn't look very happy. There was no way we were going to be doing any math for the rest of the day.

Cantaloupe

Saturday Night Live is a cool TV show. It's on at night on Saturday, and it's live. So it has the perfect name. Usually, I'm not allowed to stay up that late, but my parents said this was a special occasion because Zack was performing with Fish Food. They even let me invite Ryan, Michael, and Neil over to watch.

Everybody was excited. In the middle of the show Fish Food came out and everybody went crazy. Zack was jumping up and down and running all over the stage while he sang "I Love Dirt." It was cool.

On Monday morning everyone was talking about it. We all told Miss Mary how awesome it was to see Zack on TV.

"Okay, settle down," said Mr. Granite. "I'm sure we all watched Miss Mary's boyfriend, Zack, on *Saturday Night Live*. It was very exciting. But now that it's over, it's time to get back to work. So please turn to page twenty-three in your math books."

Oh, well, it was fun while it lasted. I knew we couldn't avoid math forever.

But you'll never believe in a million hundred years what happened at that moment.

Zack climbed in the window!

"Oh *no*!" Mr. Granite said, throwing his hands up in the air. "I give up."

"Zack!" shouted Miss Mary.

"Mary!" shouted Zack.

"I missed you!"

"I missed you, too!"

That's when the smooching began. Ugh, disgusting!

"Those two are *so* romantic!" said Andrea.

"You were awesome on TV the other night!" Ryan told Zack. "We all watched."

"Can I have your autograph?" asked Michael.

"Sure," Zack said. "I'm sorry to interrupt the class again, Mr. Granite."

"What else is new?" asked Mr. Granite.

"A lot!" Zack said. "After the show was over, a guy came into our dressing room and signed us to a record deal. Next week we're going to make our first album. We're getting T-shirts and posters, too. They're even going to make me into a bobble head statue!"*

"I'm so proud of you, Zack!" said Miss Mary.

"But here's the *big* news," Zack told Miss Mary. "Fish Food is going on a worldwide concert tour, and . . . I want *you* to come with us, Mary."

"WOW!" we all said, which is "MOM" upside down.

---

*Bobble head statues are cool.

"But . . . I promised to be a student teacher for a year," Miss Mary said. "It wouldn't be fair to Mr. Granite if I left."

"It would be fair! It would be fair!" Mr. Granite said. "Go!"

Then Zack got down on one knee in front of Miss Mary.

"Oh no!" yelled Andrea. "He's getting down on one knee!"

"I think I'm gonna cry!" yelled Emily.

"What's the big deal?" I said. "He must have dropped his contact lens or something."

Zack took a little box out of his pocket.

"I can't believe it!" Andrea shrieked. "He's got a little box!"

"So what?" I said. "He probably keeps his contact lenses in there."

All the girls were freaking out. What is their problem?

Zack opened the little box.

"Mary," Zack said, "will you marry me?"

"EEEEEEEEEEEEEEEK!" all the girls screamed. "He asked her to marry him!"

"That's *so* romantic!" Andrea said.

Oh. I guess he didn't keep contact lenses in the box after all.

Zack took a ring out of the box. Miss Mary started crying, which is what girls always do when you ask them to marry you. Nobody knows why.

"What about Daddy?" asked Miss Mary. "He doesn't approve of you."

"Old man Klutz can't keep us apart," Zack said. "If he won't give us his blessing, we can elope."

"But he would be *heartbroken*," Miss Mary said. "We can't elope!"

"What does melon have to do with it?" I asked.

"Quiet, Arlo!" said Andrea.

"Oh, why not?" Miss Mary said. "Yes, I'll marry you, Zack! Yes! Yes! Yes! Of *course* I'll marry you!"

Miss Mary put on the ring and smooched with Zack. All the girls were freaking out.*

Mr. Granite was trying to get the girls to calm down. That's when the weirdest thing in the history of the world happened.

I'm not going to tell you what it is.

Okay, okay, I'll tell you.

But you have to read the next chapter first. So nah-nah-nah boo-boo on you.

---

*As if nobody ever got married before in the history of the world, right?

79

Talking Turkey

Right after Miss Mary said she would marry Zack, the most amazing thing happened: *another* guy started climbing in the window!

"Who's *that* guy?" Michael asked.

"Quick, Zack!" Miss Mary said. "Hide in the bloody cloakroom!"

"It's like Grand Central Station in here!" Mr. Granite said as Zack ran into the cloakroom. "Doesn't anybody use doors anymore?"

The guy who climbed in the window was dressed in a jacket and tie. He carried a briefcase.

"Excuse me," the guy said, "is this Ella Mentry School?"

"Yes," Mr. Granite replied. "Who are you? What are you doing in my classroom?"

"Allow me to introduce myself," the guy said as he handed Mr. Granite a card. "My name is Joe Navark. I'm with the Hoover Vacuum Cleaner Company."

"What?!" said Mr. Granite. "I don't need

a vacuum cleaner! Get out of here! We're supposed to be doing math."

"I'm not selling vacuum cleaners," the guy said. "I'm looking for a young man named Zack. I was told I might find him here."

Mr. Granite slapped his own forehead with the palm of his hand.

"Zack is my boyfriend!" said Miss Mary, showing off her new ring. "We're going to get married."

"He's in there," Mr. Granite muttered,

pointing to the cloakroom.

The vacuum cleaner guy opened the cloakroom door. Zack was standing there.

"It's you!" the vacuum cleaner guy said to Zack. "The lead singer of Fish Food! You were terrific on *Saturday Night Live.*"

"Thank you!" said Zack.

"Tell me," the vacuum cleaner guy asked Zack, "did you write that song 'I Love Dirt'?"

"I sure did," Zack replied.

"Well, I love it!" the vacuum cleaner guy told Zack. "And I think your song would be perfect to go with the TV commercials for our new line of vacuum cleaners."

"Are you serious?" Zack asked.

"Sure!" the vacuum cleaner guy said. "Picture this. We'll have a cartoon vacuum cleaner running around a house while it sings 'I Love Dirt.' It will sell millions of vacuums!"

Zack and Miss Mary went "WOW," which is "MOM" upside down.

"Okay," the vacuum cleaner guy said. "Let's talk turkey."

"What do turkeys have to do with vacuum cleaners?" I asked. "Turkey's don't talk. Are you going to vacuum up a bunch of dead turkeys?"

"'Talking turkey' means talking about *money*, Arlo," Andrea told me.

"Oh," I said, "I knew that."

"How much are you going to pay Zack for his song?" asked Miss Mary.

"How does a million dollars sound to you?" asked the vacuum cleaner guy.

WHAT?!

"Two million would sound a lot better," Miss Mary said.

"Okay," the vacuum cleaner guy said. "Two million. But that's as high as I can go."

Zack shook hands with the vacuum cleaner guy. Everybody was freaking out.

But suddenly, there were footsteps in the hall.

"It's Mr. Klutz!" Neil the nude kid yelled.

"Quick!" Miss Mary said. "Hide in the cloakroom! Both of you!"

Zack and the vacuum cleaner guy ran into the cloakroom right before Mr. Klutz came in.

"I just wanted to see how you were making out, Mary," Mr. Klutz said.

Ew, disgusting!

"Daddy, I have wonderful news!" said Miss Mary. "Zack and I are getting married!"

"What?!" said Mr. Klutz. "You know how I feel about that, Mary. I won't allow you to marry Zack until he shows that he can earn enough money to support you."

"He can, Daddy!" Miss Mary said

excitedly. "After Zack was on *Saturday Night Live*, he signed a record contract. He's going to make an album and go on tour. And a guy from a vacuum cleaner company is going to pay Zack two million dollars for 'I Love Dirt'!"

"That *is* wonderful news!" said Mr. Klutz. "Where is Zack? I want to congratulate him."

"He's in the cloakroom," said Miss Mary, "with the guy from the vacuum cleaner company."

"What are they doing in there?" asked Mr. Klutz.

"It's a long story," said Mr. Granite.

Miss Mary opened the door to the

cloakroom. Zack and the vacuum cleaner guy came out.

"I'm the principal here," Mr. Klutz said. "Is it true that you're going to pay Zack two million dollars for 'I Love Dirt'?"

"Yes! Here's the check!" the vacuum cleaner guy said.

He showed the check to Mr. Klutz. We all crowded around to look. That check

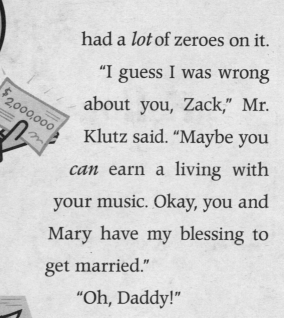

had a *lot* of zeroes on it.

"I guess I was wrong about you, Zack," Mr. Klutz said. "Maybe you *can* earn a living with your music. Okay, you and Mary have my blessing to get married."

"Oh, Daddy!"

Miss Mary started hugging and kissing Mr. Klutz. Mr. Klutz started hugging and kissing Zack. Zack started hugging and kissing the vacuum cleaner guy.

All that hugging and kissing was really gross. I thought I was gonna throw up.

Halloween

Zack and Miss Mary decided to get married on Halloween, and Mr. Klutz said they could have the wedding right in our school playground. He even got our crossing guard, Mr. Louie, to marry them because he used to be a judge.

It was a great day. All the teachers and

parents were there. Even the
vacuum cleaner guy was there.
All the kids, of course, came to
school in their costumes.

First we had a big parade
around the block. There
were cowboys, and
pumpkins, and
spacemen, and
superheroes,
and witches,
and goblins.
All the parents
were taking pic-
tures and videos. Then we had a big candy
party in the playground. I stuffed my face
with chocolate.

After the party Mr. Klutz told every-body to sit down on chairs that were set up near the monkey bars. I sat with the guys. Andrea and her girly friends sat in the row behind us.

Mr. Louie stood in front of every-body. Zack marched halfway down the aisle next to Mr. Klutz. They were all dressed up in black tuxedos. Then our music teacher, Mr. Loring, started play-ing that "Here Comes the Bride" song on an organ.

Miss Mary came down the aisle in a white gown. Yes, it was *white*! All the girls were oohing and ahhing at how pretty she looked. Zack took Miss Mary's hand,

and they walked the rest of the way down the aisle together. Everybody got quiet. You could hear a pin drop.*

"Dearly beloved," Mr. Louie said, "we are gathered here today to join this man and this woman in blah blah blah blah blah blah blah blah blah blah blah blah blah blah blah blah blah blah blah blah blah blah blah blah blah blah blah blah blah blah blah blah blah blah blah blah blah . . ."

He said a bunch of lovey-dovey stuff, but I wasn't paying attention. Mr. Louie went on and on for like a million hundred minutes, until he finally said . . .

*In fact, I think I heard one drop. But I didn't pick it up. Why should I? I didn't drop it.

"I now pronounce you husband and wife. You may kiss the bride."

Zack and Miss Mary started smooching. It was a real Kodak moment, even though kissing is disgusting.

"Isn't this romantic, Arlo?" Andrea

whispered to me. "Maybe when we grow up, you and I will get married."

"Over my dead body," I replied.

"Oooooh!" Ryan said. "A.J. just agreed to marry Andrea after he's dead! They must be in *love*!"

"When is your dead body gonna get married?" asked Michael.

After the wedding was over, Mr. Klutz got up on the stage.

"And now, ladies and gentlemen, I would like to introduce my favorite band . . . Fish Food!"

Zack and his band got up onstage.

"I love dirt! I love dirt! I love dirt! I love dirt!" Zack started chanting.

We all started chanting "I love dirt" while Zack rapped the rest of the song. He was running around and jumping up and down. It was cool.

Zack handed the microphone to Mr. Klutz, and he started yelling into it:

"I love dirt! I love dirt! I love dirt! I love dirt!"

Then Zack pulled the vacuum cleaner guy up on the stage and handed him the microphone.

"I love dirt! I love dirt! I love dirt! I love dirt!"

All the kids were jumping up and down. The teachers were dancing. Zack and the vacuum cleaner guy started playing bongos on Mr. Klutz's head. It was hilarious. Everybody was going nuts. And we got to see it live and in person.

You should have been there!

12

A Bathroom Emergency

After it was all over, Fish Food and Zack and Miss Mary got into their tour bus. It said **JUST MARRIED** on it. Somebody had tied a bunch of cans and stuff to the back bumper. What's up with that? Then they all waved good-bye and drove away. Mr. Klutz had tears in his eyes. Everybody else was really happy. Especially Mr. Granite.

That's when I realized something. I had to go to the bathroom *really* badly!

I was going to wait until I got home, but it was an emergency. I went into the school and ran down the hall to the boys' bathroom.

"Is anybody in here?" I asked as I pushed open the door, just to be on the safe side. I wasn't taking any chances, ever since the last time.

There was nobody in the bathroom. I went into one of the stalls. I did what I had to do and flushed the toilet. But that's when the weirdest thing in the history of the world happened.

The toilet *next to mine* flushed!

I figured they must be testing out the new automatic toilets again. I looked under the wall into the stall next to mine. And you'll never believe in a million hundred years what I saw in there.

It was a ghost!

A ghost was sitting on the toilet! I was freaking out!

"Who . . . are . . . you?" I asked.

"Who do I look like?" the ghost said. "I'm a ghost."

"You're a *real* ghost?"

"Of course I'm a real ghost," the ghost said.

"I didn't know ghosts use the bathroom," I said.

"Now you know," said the ghost.

"Do you eat kids for lunch?" I asked.

"No."

"Good."

"We eat kids for *dinner*," said the ghost. "And soon it will be dinnertime."

AHHHHHHHHHHHHHHHHHHHH!

I ran out of there. And I'm not going back ever again. I'm going to Antarctica to live with the penguins. Penguins are cool. And I don't think they have any ghosts in Antarctica. Or at least they don't have any in their bathrooms.

❀

Well, that's pretty much the way it happened. Maybe the boys' bathroom in our school really is haunted. Maybe we'll get another student teacher. Maybe people will stop climbing in the windows and hiding in the cloakroom. Maybe now that they're married, Miss Mary and Zack will stop smooching all the time. Maybe the Fish Food album will be a big success. Maybe Zack will teach us how to snorkel in a bog. Maybe people in England will stop saying "bloody" all the time. Maybe people will start calling sausage "sausage." Maybe Superman will zap Batman with his heat vision. Maybe Andrea will make a movie about how to be annoying. Maybe Mr. Granite will buy a new vacuum cleaner. Maybe I'll get one of Zack's bobble head statues. Maybe with Zack gone, Mr. Granite will finally be able to teach his math lesson.

But it won't be easy!